:ᚠᛟᚱ·ᛟᚢᚱ·ᚠᚨᛏᚢᚱᛗ:ᚦᛗ·ᚲᛁᚺᛗᛞᚱᚠᛟᚱᚲ:

Ϝor our Ϝuture:

Our Children

:ᚠᛟᚱ·ᛟᚢᚱ·ᚠᚨᛏᚢᚱᛗ:ᚦᛗ·ᚲᛁᚺᛗᛞᚱᚠᛟᚱᚲ:

Kindertales: Stories Old And New For The Children of the Folk

Stories © Heidi Graw, John Mainer, Freydis Heimdallson
Interior Art © Freydis Heimdallson
Edited by Freydis Heimdallson
Cover Art and Design © Freydis Heimdallson

Proceeds from the sale of this book to benefit the non-profit Heathen
Freehold Society.

Visit us online at http://bc-freehold.org

Published by
The Freyr's Press
Heathen Freehold Society

KINDERTALES

Stories Old and New for the Children of the Folk

Old Stories Told Anew

Hiuki and Bil

By Heidi Graw

Once upon a time, there was a little boy named Hiuki and a pretty girl named Bil. They had to work all night long carrying pails of water.

"I'm so tired!" cried Hiuki as he dragged his feet along the path.

"My arms cannot carry this heavy pail much longer," complained Bil as she stumbled and spilled water all over the ground.

"Why, you lazy children!" yelled their angry father, "Pick up those pails before I box your ears!"

He was about to harm his children, when Mani, driving his chariot that carries the moon, appeared from behind a silver cloud. He stopped and commanded the moonlight to freeze the father in place so he could not move a muscle.

The children stood gaping at this amazing sight. Mani grinned and asked, "Would you both like to hop in my chariot and go for a ride?"

"Of course, we will!" they shouted happily. And swift as can be, they jumped into the chariot to escape into the nighttime sky.

As for the father they left behind, when Sunna drove by in the morning with her chariot that carries the sun, the father warmed and regretted what he had done. To this day, he cries buckets full of tears.

As for Hiuki and Bil, they, to this day, play and dance around the moon. That is why you see the moon wax and wane.

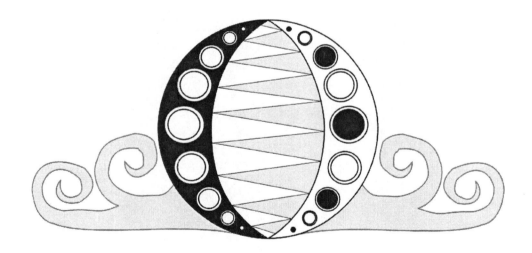

Freya's Necklace

By Heidi Graw

Once upon a time, the beautiful goddess Freya looked with dismay at her jewellery box. "I am so bored of these old jewels. I've had them forever." She sighed as she let a golden necklace slip from her hand back into the box. Ilse, Freya's servant maid, closed the box and tucked it away inside a chest of drawers.

"Perhaps, my Lady, you could ask the dwarves to make something new for you?" offered Ilse.

"Why, Ilse, that's a very good idea!" exclaimed Freya. "Odin will be hosting a party soon. I can show off a new necklace then. Or, maybe a fabulous ring! What do you think, Ilse?"

"Well, my Lady, I think a necklace would go very nicely with that new dress Amma sewed for you," said Ilse.

"A necklace it shall be!" grinned Freya. "Hurry, Ilse! Fetch my falcon cloak. I need to instruct the dwarves if they are to have a new necklace ready for me in time for the party."

Freya snatched her feathered cloak from her servant, draped it over her shoulders and flew quickly high up in the air to travel to the land where the dwarves live.

"Good morning, Dvalin." said Freya.

Amazed at seeing the exalted goddess appear so suddenly before him, Dvalin dropped his hammer and stumbled awkwardly to bow before her. "Good morning, your Highness. What a pleasant surprise. Please forgive the dirt and grime of my smithy, but you know what it's like..."

"Oh, never mind, Dvalin," said Freya as she folded up her cloak. "I haven't come to inspect the smithy, but I would very much like for you to make me a new golden necklace. Perhaps one with pretty jewels? Can you make one up in time for Odin's party?"

"Oh, to be sure, my Lady." said Dvalin, "I'll get the others to help. We will create the most beautiful necklace that I'm sure will be the envy of all."

Freya smiled and bent lower to Dvalin, "And what would you want in return? You already have all the gold nuggets you can possibly need. You have jewels, too. Is there something I can give you that you don't already have?"

"Hmmm..." pondered Dvalin, "I will need Brock and Sindri to help me create this necklace. Could the fair Lady grant us each at least one wish?"

"One wish each? That's all?" asked Freya.

"Yes, one wish each," confirmed Dvalin.

"Surely that is a small price to pay for a new necklace. You have a deal, Dvalin. One wish each it is." And with the deal properly sealed, Freya whisked off to return home to Asgard.

"Hmmm...." puzzled Dvalin, "Hey, Brock and Sindri! Our lovely Freya would like us to make a new necklace for her. I think we should make the most beautiful one that we've ever made. Have you any ideas as to the design?

Brock and Sindri both shook their heads. All three dwarves stood around and thought. And thought. And thought.... They had run out of ideas.

"I wish I had an idea for a new necklace, " said Dvalin. And before he could say another word, a new idea popped into his head. "Oh rats!" exclaimed Dvalin, "I just used up my wish!"

Brock and Sindri laughed and laughed. They couldn't believe Dvalin was so foolish to squander his one wish. But, a deal was a deal. He made a wish and it was granted. Dvalin had come up with a most beautiful design for the necklace. Then Brock got busy building up the fire to melt down the golden nuggets. He ran back and forth with more and more wood. The fire got hotter and hotter. Brock became very thirsty. And as he put the last load of wood on the burning hot coals, he wiped his forehead and exclaimed, "I wish I had a drink of water!" And before he had time to say another word, a glass of water was in his hand.

"Oh, rats!" he exclaimed, "I just squandered my one wish! I'm such a fool!" Now, it was Dvalin and Sindri's turn to laugh and laugh and laugh.

Dvalin then turned sombre and instructed Sindri: "Now, you are the only one left who can make a wish. Take great care of what you say. If it's a wish, it will come true."

Sindri took the warning to heart and pressed his lips tightly together as he busied himself with setting the jewels into the newly-forged golden necklace. He worked intently and diligently. He didn't allow his thoughts to wander. And he refused to speak. He said not a word. Nothing. He worked and worked until all the work was done. The necklace was so beautiful that the one word he allowed himself to say was, "Brisingamen." He had named the necklace.

As soon as Freya received word her necklace was done, she once again set out to meet the dwarves. "Well, dear friends," said Freya, "I have already granted two wishes." She smiled as she thought about Dvalin and Brock's foolishness. "So, Sindri, it seems to me that I owe you one wish. Have you thought about it, yet?"

Sindri blushed a deep purple red, "Yes, my Lady. I do have one wish."

"What is it, dear Sindri?" asked Freya.

"I-I-I-," stuttered Sindri, "I mean, if it's not too much trouble, I wish for a kiss from you. Yes. That's what I wish. I wish for a kiss." Sindri could scarcely look at that gracious and beautiful goddess. He had always been really shy.

Freya smiled and bent lower. Sindri raised up his face and pursed his lips. Freya leaned closer and planted a very soft and sweet kiss on Sindri's forehead! Having fulfilled her end of the bargain, Freya took the necklace and flew off wearing her feathery garb. Dvalin and Brock stood giggling, while Sindri appeared very disappointed. But, a kiss was a kiss. A wish had been fulfilled.

Had you been one of the dwarves, what would you have wished for?

How Sleipnir Came To Be

By Heidi Graw

Once upon a time, Coal-muzzle, the young billy-goat, was nibbling at some tasty greens growing along the outer edges of the Asgard walls. He was very hungry. He nibbled and nibbled and nibbled until he went almost all the way around the huge towering walls, when all of a sudden, he found himself nibbling at the edges of an old smelly coat.

"Whoa there, Coal-muzzle! Watch it, will you? That's my coat you're nibbling on." complained the dwarf Andvari.

"Phui," spat out Coal-muzzle. "It tastes like old rotten fish. What are you doing here anyway?" he asked.

"Ah, it's a long story," sighed Andvari. "Remember how I used to live like a fish in the Rhine River? Well, I lost my job guarding the gold. And that Loki! Darn it all! He took my ring that guaranteed my wealth. I haven't been able to find a decent job since. Now look at me! I've been assigned to watch this unfinished gate that leads into Asgard."

"Why is it unfinished, Andvari?" asked Coal-muzzle.

"Loki's doing, that's why!" grumbled the dwarf. "He and his bright ideas about how to get this wall built for nothing...no payment...not even for a small piece of gold." Andvari muttered and cussed at his bad luck.

"Gee, Andvari. That's really too bad," sympathized Coal-muzzle. "But, what about this gate? Why isn't it finished? And why did the gods assign you to guard it? You look a little too short to do a very good job of it."

"Oh, hush up before I take those little horns of yours and skewer you to these walls!" threatened the dwarf.

"Calm down, Andvari," said the billy-goat. "Can I take a peek inside? I heard Asgard is really one fantastic place."

"No, you cannot!" blasted Andvari. "Go on with you! Come on, get away from here!"

"All right," said Coal-muzzle, looking rather dejected, "But at least tell me why this gate is unfinished. Will you do that?" he pleaded.

"Hmmm..." grumbled the dwarf, "Okay. But sit quietly and I'll tell you what happened."

Coal-muzzle obeyed and nuzzled close to Andvari who sat down near the unfinished entrance to Asgard. The little goat placed his coal black nose on the dwarf's lap and gazed contentedly at Andvari's beard. He was thinking about nibbling at those curly tufts of hair, but remembered the taste of Andvari's coat. He decided against it and, instead, listened attentively to Andvari's story:

A long, long time ago, the gods worried about how best to protect Asgard from the giants. While they sat in council to discuss this issue, a builder, from seemingly nowhere, came to offer his services. He bragged he could build a fortification so strong and so large that no mountain or frost giants could tear it down. He also insisted he could build this wall within three seasons. But, he demanded that if he succeeded in finishing the job within that time frame, he wanted Freya as a wife and wished to have the sun and the moon also.

Freya was the first to protest. She pointed out that she was already married and had no wish to leave Asgard with someone she didn't even know, much less not even love. She looked with alarm at her husband, Odur. He laughed, leaned over to her and quietly whispered, "Now, don't worry, Freya. Do you really think I'd let you run off with that two-bit construction worker?"

"Trust me," chimed in Loki. He, too, leaned over to Freya and whispered, "Let's agree to the terms so that we can have that wall built. I'll swear you won't have to marry this guy."

"But what about us?" interrupted Mani, "Sol and I will end up drawing empty carriages. What good will these be without the sun and moon to pull across the heavens? Little Bil and young Hiuki would also end up dancing around in the dark. They could fall out of the carriage!"

"Not to mention everything else being shrouded in darkness if we let the giants take control of the sun and moon," added Sol. "Surely, we can't risk that, can we?"

After much deliberation, the gods counter-demanded the builder construct the walls during the one season of winter. And if, by that first day of summer he had failed to finish the job, he would have to forfeit his payment. The builder agreed and then asked for permission to use his stallion Svadilfaeri to assist him with this task. Loki pressed for an agreement to these terms. He believed it would be impossible for the builder to succeed.

When the first day of winter arrived, the builder enthusiastically set to his work. His stallion hauled massive stones from the nearby hillside at night, while the builder set the stones in place during the day. The Aesir were very much impressed by the stallion's strength and by the speed the project was progressing. And as winter passed, the walls were rapidly raised. They were so high and strong that it appeared certain no giants could storm over them. And with just three days left before the first day of summer, the gateway to Asgard was about to take shape. The gods worried that they might lose Freya to this builder and that the heavens would no longer have the sun and the moon.

They blamed Loki for making this terrible agreement and threatened that if he did not do everything in his power to stop this builder from succeeding in finishing up the fortification, they would attack Loki and kill him. Loki promised to find a way out of this deal.

That same evening, when the builder was about to continue with his work, his stallion noticed a beautiful mare in the nearby woods. It was Loki in disguise. The mare whinnied and neighed. Her soft brown eyes gazed lovingly at Svadilfaeri. Then, with a swing of her rump and a swish of her tail, she galloped off into the deeper woods, Svadilfaeri running close behind her. The builder, frustrated and angry, followed. That night, no work was done. The following day not much more was accomplished.

The builder realized he was not going to get the work finished in time and flew into a giant rage. The Aesir then discovered the builder was actually an evil mountain giant. They called upon Thor to kill him. Thor had been away fighting the wicked trolls in a far-off distant land. And when word reached him the Aesir needed help, he quickly hopped into his chariot and thundered across the skies. When he caught sight of the giant, he hurled his mighty hammer, Miolnir. The giant ducked and hurled back mighty stones. Thor veered out of the way just in time. Again, he threw his hammer. Again, the giant threw stones. Thor's two goats joined in this mighty battle. Tooth-cracker and Tooth-gnasher leapt at the giant and pinned him down. Thor's hammer struck the giant's head and crushed it. That evil mountain giant finally lay dead.

The Aesir cheered Thor's victory and celebrated in grand style. The goats, too, were not forgotten and received their own reward: an extra helping of very special greens. "Did you know Thor's goats are my cousins?" interjected Coal-muzzle. "When I grow up, I'm going to be just like them. Brave and strong."

"Ssshhhh," hissed Andvari, "I told you to be quiet. Now hush and let me continue..."

In the meantime, Loki had been galloping around as that pretty mare. His intention was to distract and lead Svadilfaeri away from the work site. But he had made himself so attractive to Svadilfaeri that the stallion quickly caught up with Loki and overtook him. A very shocked Loki soon discovered he was pregnant. But what was even worse, there was no way he could turn himself back into his normal shape. Loki had no choice but to abide his time and wait until he, as a mare, gave birth to a foal. It was grey and had eight legs, and was the best horse ever born. He was the swiftest and strongest. Loki gave this horse to Odin as a present to make up for all the trouble and worries that he had caused the Aesir. And this is how Sleipnir came to be.

The little goat roused himself from Andvari's lap and added, "It also explains why the gate to Asgard was never finished. By the way, how did you come to be the guard for this gate?"

"Never mind," replied Andvari. "That's a whole 'nother story." And thus dismissed, young Coal-muzzle scampered home to his own straw bed.

The Story of the Langobards

By Heidi Graw

Once upon a time, late at night, young Coal-muzzle the billy goat had trouble sleeping. Something strange was in the air and he wanted to find out what it was. So, he snuck out of his shelter and wandered up the path leading to Asgard.

Andvari, the dwarf, was fast asleep at his post. Coal-muzzle quickly tip-tapped past him and made his way to Fensalir, the palace where the great Goddess Queen Frigga lives. Her home was still lit brightly and the door was slightly ajar. Young Coal-muzzle poked his little head inside the palace and saw the heavenly Queen still spinning wool at this late hour. Every so often she looked over at her husband Odin who was fast asleep on the couch. She would sigh and return back to her spinning.

There were many fluffs of wool floating around in the room. Some floated out of the open windows, others gathered at the corners of the ceiling in the room. Strands of twisted wool were coiling up in the basket on the floor next to the gracious Goddess. A wisp of wool landed on Coal-muzzle's nose and caused him to sneeze. "Ah-ah-choo! Ah-choo!"

Frigga quickly looked over to find Coal-muzzle trying to stop himself from sneezing by burying his muzzle in the soft rug that lay at the entrance. "Coal-muzzle! You silly little goat! What are you doing up so late at night?"

"Oh, oh, ah-choo!" sneezed Coal-muzzle in a panic. "I'm so sorry... I couldn't sleep. I didn't mean to disturb you. Ah-choo!"

"Ssshhh, Coal-muzzle! You'll wake up Odin with all that noise!" scolded the great Queen. "Come over here and use this old hanky."

Thoroughly embarrassed, Coal-muzzle tip-tapped over towards Frigga and allowed the great Queen to wipe his nose. "Now, you sit right here and tell me just why you're out this late at night," the Queen firmly demanded.

"I couldn't sleep. There is something strange in the air," explained the young goat. "Besides, Tooth-gnasher was making too much noise grinding his teeth. So, I thought I'd take a walk around outside. Why are you still up so late?" Coal-muzzle looked up at the many fluffs floating around in the room.

"Oh, I have a big problem, Coal-muzzle," sighed the Queen. "The Winilers and the Vandals are preparing to fight each other in the morning.

32

Odin promised the Vandals the victory, but I want the Winilers to win. Of course, Odin didn't quite say who he wants to see win this battle. He merely told me that he'd assign victory to those who he would see first in the morning. And as you can see, when Odin wakes in the morning, he will see the Vandals! What I need to do is turn his couch around so that the first people he'd see are the Winilers. But, the couch is too heavy to move, especially with Odin still sleeping on it!" The Queen looked over at her sleeping husband and let out a deep and unhappy sigh.

"Oh," was Coal-muzzle's small reply. He had no idea as to what to suggest. He wasn't sure if he even should.

Alas, the Queen returned to her spinning. Coal-muzzle laid himself down beside her and began nibbling at the wool in her basket. He nibbled and nibbled until his belly was quite full and then ... he burped!

"Oh, my goodness! Coal-muzzle! What did you do?" cried Frigga. "That was wool I spun for Dag's new morning cloak! He wanted something new to wear.... and you ate it all up! How could you?"

"Oh, I'm so sorry," winced the young billy goat. "I didn't even realize I was doing that," and crawled under Frigga's chair to hide his shame.

Frigga got up and went down on her knees to try to pull the young goat from under the chair. "You have no idea what you did, do you? This is magic wool I spun! Who knows what will happen now that you ate it!" She frantically tried to grasp the leg of the goat so she could pull him out from under her chair.

"Burp!" belched the little goat and, to Frigga's amazement, the chair lifted up quite on its own.

Coal-muzzle was stuck to its bottom and was rising along with it.

"Well, I'll be..." gasped the heavenly Queen. "I think I know how I can move Odin's couch around." And with that, she grabbed Coal-muzzle's hind legs and pulled him gently down along with the chair and wiggled him out from under it. She clung fast to the little goat and could feel herself being pulled upward, too. With great effort, she summoned up her own weight and remained firmly planted on the ground. "Whew!" she exclaimed, squeezing the goat until he burped once more.

"What are you going to do to me?" wailed Coal-muzzle. "Ouch! Don't squeeze me so hard," he complained.

"Hush! I have an idea and I need you to co-operate," replied Frigga while she loosened her grip on the little goat. "I'm going to put you under

Odin's couch and when it lifts up, I'll turn it around. After that, I think I'll just let you fly around outside. Would you like that?" She grinned as Coal-muzzle's face shrank in terror.

"I don't want to be a flying goat!" he cried.

"Why not?" asked Frigga. "Both Tooth-gnasher and Tooth-cracker can fly. I thought you wanted to be just like them? Besides, I don't know how I can undo what you did to yourself. Maybe in due time the effects will wear off. But at this moment, I need you to co-operate with me."

Frigga then tucked young Coal-muzzle under the couch and when it lifted off the floor, she turned it the other way around. Odin didn't skip a beat of his rhythmic snoring and remained sound asleep.

And when the great Goddess pulled the young goat from under the couch, she took him outside and with a strong rope she tied him to a sturdy fence post. There, young Coal-muzzle spent a very unhappy night.

In the meantime, the Winilers had received instructions to round up their women and station them in battle array. The ladies had been told to dress in battle gear and wear their hair carefully combed forward in the manner of long beards.

When Odin awoke and gazed outside, he exclaimed in surprise, "What Longbeards are those?" Frigga smiled with deep satisfaction. Those Langobards gained a victory and went on to become the people of Lombardy.

And the fate of young Coal-muzzle? After spending such a dreadful night floating in the air while clinging to a rope, the magic effects did eventually wear off. He swore never again to nibble on strands of wool... no matter who had spun it.

Original Tales

Ostara and the Dance of the Bunnies

By John Mainer

In the dawn of the age of man, when the tribes of men were new formed, and taking their first halting steps upon Midgard, Ostara was often seen bringing the springtime to field, forest and fen.

The tribes of men watched with amazement as Ostara would walk upon the earth, and it would rouse to wakefulness behind her. As she walked did the first shoots push aside the snowmelt rubble and greet sweet Sunna's sunshine; as she smiled the first flowers would blossom, and the air turn sweet and fresh. At her side flew a white bird, graceful and joyous. Always the song of her companion bird would call the spring birds from the far south, to return again to the northlands, and with them bring the ocean breezes that fire the hearts of young men.

The tribes of men were thankful to Ostara, and wished to give thanks to her in a way that was pleasing to her, and for this, they watched the rabbits. All winter long, Ostara sleeps, for she cannot abide the touch of Ymir's get, and flees the coming of the snow. When Sunna turns her face again to the world, and the snows and Frost Giants retreat back to their mountain fastness, the rabbits call Ostara to wake. In the spring, the rabbits dance. Upon the earth in wild abandon, the rabbits wassail hard, and in their joyous measure stir the sleeping Ostara, for her return brings the spring.

Year on year Ostara woke to the dancing of the rabbits, year on year her graceful companion bird would watch the dancing rabbits, and hunger to join their measure. In a year known only in song as the year of the rabbit, came the great change. In that year was grown a rabbit of heroic proportions, a champion of his breed who scoffed at foxes, and defied falcons in his strength. His eye was taken with the gentle bird of Ostara, for her grace and beauty called to him as no she-rabbits could. Come the spring in the year of change, he danced for her. He danced with the wild abandon of his breed, he danced with the fire that Freya grants to lovers, and the rage Odin grants the doomed.

It was a dance of dances, from a champion fired by a love that could not be, and it cast a spell more powerful than any spaewitch's rune. While Ostara laughed at the display, her companion watched transfixed; her bird eyes fixed like a hunting falcon's, her head bobbing with the measure. No longer able to contain herself, she flew from Ostara's shoulder and lit upon the ground. At first stately in feathered grace, then swiftly in wing-fluffing abandon she danced with her feathered suitor. Round and round they danced, as wild as any Alfar circle, and lit by Freya's fire.

No longer smiling, Ostara watched her companion dance with her furred lord. It was clear her bird had lost its heart to this rabbit prince. Striding forward to the circle, Ostara halted the dancers with a glance. The rabbits trembled before the gaze of the goddess, but the champion stood forth fearless in his love, the white bird at his side. Ostara smiled softly, and the bird bowed deeply and sang a song of love: love for a friend of long centuries, love of a woman for a man; love that would trade eternity for fulfillment. Ostara heard the song, and her heart was moved. She knelt and kissed her companion, and when she rose again, there was only a shining she-rabbit in a pile of soft feathers.

When Ostara walked away, the rabbit champion took his new-won love into the warren, and her new home.

As the snow retreated, the rabbits began to dance again, to wake Ostara. In the wake of the Year of Change, Ostara woke sadly. She walked upon the world alone, and her coming brought no life; for her heart was heavy. The tribes of man were worried, for the spring brought no life, and the priests and wise women said to watch the rabbits, for they held the secret of this dire spring. The fastest and best hunters coursed the land, not to kill, but to watch the rabbits for the secret of the dire spring.

When Ostara reached the lands of the champion, and her lost companion, she beheld all of the rabbits in a dancing circle, and in the center two rabbits stood before a mound of feathers. As Ostara neared, the dancing rabbits parted, bowing her in. As she gazed with sadness on the aging of her now mortal former companion, the two rabbits stood aside showing Ostara the secret they concealed. Inside the nest of feathers were a dozen eggs, one of which was busy trying to hatch a wiggling little bunny.

As the bunny burst forth with a triumphant *cheep!* Ostara's heart melted like the departing snow, and she began to laugh; picking up this flop-eared chick, she danced a merry measure with her rabbit folk. As she danced the spring burst forth, the field erupted with flowers, the trees grew bright with new growth, and the sky full of song from the returning birds.

The hunters carried word of this back to the several tribes of men, and it was whispered amongst the wise how not only the dance, but an offering of eggs won Ostara's heart and brought forth the spring.

Henceforth Ostara was honoured by the tribes of man with offerings of eggs in springtime. Here ends our tale for today. The story of her new companion, Ostara's Bunny, is one for another day, but a tale worthy of singing none the less.

Ostara's Bunny

By John Mainer

For as long as Ostara's rest in Asgard was defended by the Yule Father's great spear, and the watchful eyes of Heimdal, so was this gift of service repaid with similar service. As the Allfather's Yuletide duties caused him to gift the good children of the world, it fell upon him to be sure that those children so gifted were remaining true in the waxing of the new year. As Ostara's bunny was idle during his mistress's slumber, he was not only free to serve, but in his boundless love for children, and winter spawned cabin fever, actually dying to do so.

So did Father Yule, great Odin himself, charge Ostara's bunny; "Seek you out the good boys and girls on Sweet Frigga's list, and see that they still keep the peace, mind their parents, work hard, and do not attempt to sell their siblings at auction." With a nod and a dash the sweet bunny sped across Asgard, blew right between startled Heimdal's legs, past two incoming Valkyries (who were used to such antics and frequently spoiled the bunny with snacks when Ostara wasn't looking), and skidded down the rainbow bridge onto Midgard. Time was short, for Ostara waked soon, and the world was broad, so he'd best be on the hop!

Down in Midgard, the pace of life was slower, and the upcoming holiday at Easter had the children at boarding school all bustling to go home; at least those with homes to go to. One little girl, named Ilsa, was an orphan, and although her Aunt and Uncle loved her, and saw to her needs, they were abroad through the Easter season, and so at school she would remain. While it was a touch boring alone at the school, some staff still remained with work to do, and so she was free to roam the whole dorm, and even lend a hand in the kitchens, for the cook was always ready for willing little hands, and had special little treats to reward them.

The rain was hammering all of North Scotland, so Ilsa had to spend the whole day indoors. The cook had gone home as they repainted the kitchen, so Ilsa did not even have work to amuse herself. Thus was Ilsa lying in the halls, singing to the echoes of her voice, and being bored to tears when Ostara's bunny found her. His magic was strong, from Ostara herself, and he passed through the walls like a hand passes through smoke; his magic was set to keep him from all eyes, so he watched her unseen as she sang, and she sighed.

Although he was ageless, he was still young at heart, and he knew this sweet girl was alone far too long. For like this sweet child he alone often waited; for his sleeping mistress all winter he bided. Unlike her he was free across Asgard to roam, in trouble and out all the winter at home. Knowing he shouldn't, but knowing he would, Ostara's bunny let his magic unveil him and boldly he stood.

Ilsa just lay there in startled surprise, as a bunny just popped out before her wee eyes. The bunny hopped up and touched her wee nose, then dashed to the corner, spun and he froze. He waited for Ilsa to rise and to run, let her get close, then took off at the run. All through the halls, up the stairs did they race, her laughter and shrieks sang the song of the chase. He hopped and he bopped until she'd run herself out, then hopped on her lap when she collapsed on the floor. Laughing and stroking her floppy eared friend, Ilsa asked shyly if she'd see him again. With a flick of his tail and the wink of an eye, the bunny patted her nose then took off through the wall. Ilsa sat startled to see how he left, for the brick walls were solid, and really quite thick.

Ilsa decided her friend had been magic, and magical bunnies were not really common. She thought and she thought, then she thought of the season, and then she knew the bunny had hopped for a reason. Ostara's bunny himself it had been, and quite an honour just to be seen. What a treat for Ostara's own bunny to stay, through the whole afternoon, asking only to play. A gift for a gift was the way of all friends, so what kind of gift could she make and how send?

Ilsa asked of the cook, and the old woman laughed, for she took it as fancy, as the dream of a lonely wee girl or a story. Still did the cook tell the story, as she knew it, of the gift of eggs for Ostara, called Easter. Ilsa begged and she pleaded, and the cook she soon melted, and pots were set forth for white eggs to be boiled. Boiled and dried, her eggs were prepared, but how now to wrap them? Ilsa fluttered and fretted, for the classrooms were closed: no wrap, no sparkles, no ribbons or glue; how was she to wrap them? What could she do? She wanted her gift to be beautifully wrapped, a way to say thanks to her floppy-eared friend. To the cook now she came with her eyes all in tears, and the little old lady took heed of her fears.

"Now the wrap," said the cook "Is to make them look bright. Well, that we can do, and do it up right." With her dyes and her inks, did she teach the sweet tot how to paint up her eggs, and to brighten them up. Happy at last, Ilsa was painting; each little egg was a wonder in making. Come the night she stowed her basked of eggs, brightly painted she left them where her bunny companion had popped in to see her.

Easter was come, and Ostara had wakened, her bunny was hopping quite joyful to see her. Her bunny beside her, she strode through the world, bringing spring to the northlands and joy in the season. When she crossed to old Scotland her bunny was distracted, she asked if there was something the matter.

Explaining quite quickly about his indiscretion, he feared he would anger his newly waked mistress. Smiling instead, Ostara did laugh, and asked to be taken to see Ilsa herself. Ostara and bunny did come to the school, just for a visit, for they had much to do. Ostara's bunny saw Ilsa's beautiful Easter gift, he was struck not just speechless, but hoppless as well. Ostara laughed to see her friend's distress, and as he looked at her and begged her help she already had a thought. "Your friend gives you thanks for her day of play, but you know we cannot tarry on this Easter day. We have a world to waken, a Spring to bring forth, but we cannot leave her lonely, of course.

"A gift, and a game," was Ostara's answer.

Ostara's Bunny thought the idea was just splendid, and began to hide eggs everywhere unattended. He hid them in corners, and under old socks, he hid them in stairwells, in old coffee pots; he hid them so his friend could seek them all day, a gift for a gift and all day to play. Ostara just watched him, and seemed quite amused. "Darling, she said, let me make one small change, for young girls are different from both you and I. " Ostara drew a breath, and then softly sighed, and twinkling surrounded the eggs in their hides. Ostara's bunny was curious, and hopped right on over; the egg was now chocolate, and sparkled all over. Knowing his mistress had got it quite right, he hopped off with a chuckle, into the dawn's light. Around all the world they worked Ostara's will, bringing the Spring through the last winter chill.

When sweet Ilsa woke, she was amazed to discover a glittering egg, in a sparkling wrapper. Knowing the gift was from her floppy-eared friend, she opened it quickly and found a surprise. This egg was of chocolate! What a treat! As the light filled her room she discovered two more, then out to the halls where she met him before. Taking her basket, she filled it right up with eggs made of chocolate, from hide and go seek!

Word of this wonder spread through the school, when the students returned and they thought it was cool. Now every Easter the children remember, and honour Ostara and bunny together. As once long ago, we all greet the Spring, but now done with chocolate, the whole world over.

The Good Goatherd and the Good Shepherd

By Freydis Heimdallson

Once upon a time, a long time ago, a shepherd lived high in the mountains. He prided himself on being a very good shepherd. He tended his sheep with care, and they grew fat on the sweet mountain grass.

One day he noticed that one of his lambs was missing. He went to search for it.

As he roamed about the mountain, looking for his lost lamb, he came upon another flock of sheep, contentedly grazing.

"Sheep!" he thought. "I thought all the sheep on this mountain were mine! I do not recognise them; still, am I not the shepherd? I will take them with me."

As he was rounding them up, a man came up. "What are you doing?" he asked the shepherd.

"I am gathering up my lost sheep," replied the shepherd.

"I am sorry to hear that you've lost your sheep," said the man, "But these aren't them. These are my sheep."

"No, these are my sheep," said the shepherd; "They've always been my sheep. They simply didn't know it."

"No, these are my sheep! Go away!"

"But do you not care for your sheep?" asked the shepherd.

"Of course I do," replied the man, irritated and confused.

"Then you will what is best for them. I am the Good Shepherd; they will be better off with me than with anyone else." And he struck the man down and left with his sheep.

Many days later, as he herded his flock across the high mountain pastures, he came across another man tending another flock. "Ah, here are more of my lost sheep!" he said.

The other man eyed him. "No; these are my sheep."

"They have always been mine," said the Good Shepherd; "And now I have come for them! I am the Good Shepherd."

"Well, I am a good shepherd, too," said the man angrily; "And I will not let you steal my sheep!"

"But you want what is best for your sheep, do you not? With me, they will thrive on the sweetest mountain grasses."

"My sheep already eat the sweetest mountain grasses; they are thriving already!"

"Ah, but the grass they eat in my care will be even sweeter!"

The man looked at the Shepherd's flock, grazing next to his own. "What, like now?"

"Yes," replied the Good Shepherd.

"So the grass they eat while in your care.."

"Will be sweeter by far than that which they now eat."

"But they're eating the same grass!"

"The grass my sheep eat is sweeter."

"Really. And why is that?"

"Because I guided them to it." And with that, the Good Shepherd struck the other man down and took his sheep.

It wasn't very much longer before the people of the village noticed that many of their men and their flocks were missing, and that the Good Shepherd's flock was strangely larger. The village elders paid him a visit.

"Many of our men are missing," they said; "And their sheep. Whereas your own flock increases daily. What do you have to say for yourself?"

"These are all my sheep," said the Good Shepherd calmly.

"There are those who would argue that."

"They are sheep; therefore they are mine. All sheep are my sheep. I am the Good Shepherd!"

"Look, you can't just go about stealing other people's sheep!"

"I am not stealing. I take only what is rightfully mine."

"Which is all sheep."

"Yes."

The elders looked at each other in consternation. "And why should they all be yours?" one asked finally.

"Because I am the Good Shepherd! Under my care, no sheep will suffer. I allow none of my sheep to die."

"Well, none of us do!"

"But you slaughter them," replied the Good Shepherd. "You take their wool and their lives and give them nothing back."

"We protect them and shelter them," replied the elders; "We ease their births and feed them well. They feed us and we keep their numbers in check so that they don't starve. We are shepherds!"

"But I am the Good Shepherd! Sheep in my care shall want for nothing. And the sheep in my care shall live forever!"

"Then... you don't slaughter them?" asked one.

"Or fleece them?" asked another.

"No."

Once again the elders looked at each other uncertainly. But then, one of them noticed the pot bubbling over the fire. "That's mutton!" he said accusingly. "And your clothes are made of wool!"

"Yes."

"Then you do fleece your sheep! And your sheep do die!"

"No," replied the Good Shepherd; "When I partake of the flesh of a sheep it becomes one with me; the sheep may die, but the Sheep continues." And he kicked them all out and shut the door.

No one knew what to do about the Good Shepherd. They tried grazing their flocks with others, but still, men disappeared, and the Good

Shepherd's flock grew larger. "How many sheep does one man need?" they wondered. "And how do we stop him from taking ours?"

One day, a young man asked his father why the Good Shepherd was taking all the sheep.

"He says they're all his," his father replied, "Because they're sheep."

"Well, we'll just see about that," said Hans, for that was his name; "I think I shall introduce him to my goats." For Hans was a goatherd.

The next morning, instead of heading to his usual pastures, he took his flute, his sling, and his goats, and went in search of the Good Shepherd. After a while he came across the edge of a vast flock grazing on the mountainside. He settled in with his goats, lay back against a warm boulder, and took out his flute. His sling he laid to hand nearby.

After a while a shadow fell over him. "My lost sheep!" a voice boomed.

Hans paused his playing but did not look up. "No, these are goats," he said, and once again set the flute to his lips.

"They look like sheep."

"They aren't," said Hans again; "They're goats."

"Prove it," said the Good Shepherd, for indeed it was he.

"Prove they're sheep," replied Hans equably.

"They have horns; their hooves are cloven. They are sheep."

"You're a bit near-sighted, aren't you?" remarked Hans. He placed a pebble in his sling and stood up.

"What's that for?"

"Ducks," replied Hans.

"Ducks? There are no ducks around here!"

"There might be," replied Hans, scanning the sky and idly spinning the sling. "A nice plump duck would make an excellent dinner. Or perhaps a goose," and he put a larger stone in his sling instead.

"Ducks be damned," growled the Good Shepherd; "Give me my sheep!"

"I can't; they're goats."

"I am the Good Shepherd; in my care no sheep will perish!"

"Then what do you eat?" asked Hans curiously.

"The sheep I consume do not die, but become one with me, and continue."

"The same might be said of the flesh I eat."

"No, for in you the flesh does not linger, but is passed through and becomes excrement."

"Fertilizer, to make the grass grow."

"The sheep I eat is not parted from me; it becomes one with me."

"Then I wonder greatly that you are not extremely fat. Or extremely constipated."

"Bah!" said the Good Shepherd. "These are my sheep; I am taking them with me!"

"You are welcome to try to take any sheep that you find here," said Hans.

The Good Shepherd glared at him, but when Hans did nothing more than twirl his sling and idly scan the skies he simply grunted and set about gathering up the goats.

However, when he stood behind them to drive them towards his own flock, instead of obediently trotting away from him, they simply scattered around him and resumed grazing. Try as he might, he could not drive them.

"What is wrong with these sheep?" he cried in frustration.

"They're not sheep; they're goats, and they're happy where they are," said Hans, spinning the sling a little faster. "Is that a goose up there?" he added.

"Bah! They are sheep, and I will have them," growled the Good Shepherd. He tried once more to drive them, but the herd was getting edgy with him prancing about in their midst; they jumped away, and the billies rolled their eyes at him.

"Fine," said the Good Shepherd, and he dove to grab a kid. "I'll move them one at a time if I have to!"

"Don't do that," said Hans; "I keep telling you, they're not sheep! They'll fight to protect themselves."

And sure enough, the kid's mother reared up, legs flailing, to drive the Good Shepherd away from her offspring. The billies reared back and butted him, their hard heads bruising flesh and cracking ribs. "Get them off!" cried the Good Shepherd in panic, and tried to kick at them. "I am the Good Shepherd!"

"And I am a good goatherd," said Hans, twirling his sling above his head, "And I too will protect my charges!" and with that, he released his sling. The rock flew hard and true, and struck the Good Shepherd between his eyes. The Good Shepherd was dead before he fell.

Hans sat back down and picked up his flute. "There, there," he called to his goats, and played a calming melody. The billies, satisfied that the threat to their little tribe was gone, soon led the herd away to graze again.

Once they had settled, Hans packed up his flute and sling, and whistled to the goats. "Come on," he called. "I know it's still early, but I've got to tell the villagers to come and get their sheep." And, not driving, but leading his goats, he headed back home.

Shoeless Pony and the Fearless Goat

By John Mainer

There was a time in the land of the Jutes when neighbour warred not with neighbour, when the ships of Dane and Swede were as apt to call in peace as raid. The wights and alfar were at peace, the crops dark and heavy, and the sky as apt for sunshine as shower. This time of idyll was ended, of course, by the arrogance of man, and the vengeance of the Aesir.

In the town of Hrafnborg lived Svalli the merchant, son of Ivar Shield-breaker, the noted reaver and sea lord. Svalli inherited his father's great wealth, his knack for trading and eye for opportunity, but none of his fierce courage or sense of honour; he was thus a man of much riches, but little fame or respect in Hrafnborg. Chief amongst Ivar's Thanes was Ragnar Odosson, called Mad Ragnar, who had won much fame through his many voyages, but unending glory when he gave his life to win Ivar free of the Byzantine fire ship that had nigh caught them in the Bosporus. Mad Ragnar was survived by his wife Helga, a noted wise woman; his two young sons, wild pups of the wolf father; and by Brita, a daughter graced with her mother's wisdom and beauty, and her father's wild spirit.

While Svalli's name was mentioned with his father's, only to say that he was "No Ivar," Brita's name was mentioned by all with both father's and mother's fame. Laughing as she coursed bareback over fences on the white stallion only she and Ragnar could ever hold, the villagers would laugh, "A true child of Mad Ragnar, that one!" and smile as they spoke. Too would they smile to see her at her mother's side called to births and foaling, for her hands were sure and judgment much spoken of.

Svalli looked to the feast of Walpurgnicht to make the fame that had long been denied him. His father was famed for his open-handed generosity, even as he was known for his adventures, and his wise judgment. Svalli, though hard to part with any coin, had hungered so long for the fame of his father; he had determined to have it, whatever the price. He had decided to strip his farms of stock, slaughtered for the feast, to have his ships bring fine wine from the southlands, that villagers had never tasted, and to gift the village with an oath ring, solid gold, and the size of a shield boss.

The ring was fine gold and fashioned like two snakes coiled about themselves, eating each other's tails. It was of fine African craftsmanship, and had been Ivar's prize possession, having been an abbot's privy rim from far Egypt. 'Twas this gift that caught fox-Loki's eye, for jest, jape and mock are his coin; more will be said of this anon.

Brita Helgasdotter had a gift to give as well; while her mother sent sweet mead by the keg, fine hams, and good bread, Brita's gift was the noblest. Brita was now a marriageable maid, and she wished no husband of less fame than her father. To that end, she offered her stallion Lightning as sacrifice for Walpurgis. The stallion was bred by Ragnar, and would allow only Ragnar and Brita to touch him; his matchless endurance and fierce nature made him the envy of princes, but he was offered only to

74

Odin, that Brita find a husband as favoured by the Allfather as was Mad Ragnar.

Walpurgnicht was well attended; the farms from the hills and fells had emptied into the town, with only mother Helga away at Vitgurdsteading, with the goodwife expecting twins. Children and thralls sported in the street, while the freemen and women showed off their best, made bargains and matches for the year ahead, and spoke of apprenticeships for the elder children. The feast itself was a wonder: kegs of wine from Svalli, and mead from Brita Helgasdotter and old Sven, bread and pies from a dozen farms, and enough meat roasting for a king's own hall.

When the time for blot had come, Brita led Lightning down for slaughter; he had ribbons in his mane, and his hooves were polished to a steel shine. As priest and assistant approached with knife and hammer, Lightning reared up and charged, scattering the holders and priests, for a time it seemed that the blood would not be the horse's that was offered. Brita leapt with all speed to grab Lightning's lead rope, and she shouted for him to be still, and his great head bowed as he nudged her gently and he held still. While the crowd had shouted and shied at the stallion's charge, three strangers had moved to the fore: an old warrior with his left face scarred blind, his fox-faced brother, and his great giant of a son. The old warrior's eye shone with admiration for the horse. "That is a worthy thing," he said.

The red-beard bellowed a laugh. "That is a worthy lass," he said. The fox faced stranger just sneered. The hammer fell, and the horse stood stunned, and with a flourish the priest's knife sang; and the blot was done with much good omen, as the sacrifice stood tall and strong till his life's blood was all spilt.

The gift of the girl was the talk of the town, as was her beauty and her outstanding courage. Hot and true in Brita flowed Ragnar's blood they said, while in Svalli old Ivar's ran thin. The fox-faced stranger flowed up to Svalli. "Have you no gift greater than hers? " he asked. With a voice as smooth as the scales of a snake, with a laugh like the crackling fire, "For without one the fame will be hers once again, and for you will be only the scorn. "

"By the gods, sir, I do!" roared Svalli with rage, as he swiftly kicked and struck at his thralls where they feasted. "Back to the hall," he screamed at them; "Fetch my gift; no more lazing for you!"

The townsmen shook their head at Svalli's poor thralls; no rest even on Walpurgsnicht. But swiftly in the wine and the mead and the dance, all memory of harshness was lost. Within an hour did the thralls then return with the ring, so heavy it took both to hold.

"Behold," said Svalli, "An Oath ring for the town, of gold and wrist thick all around. Will this please the gods on this Walpurgis Night," he asked; "Is this not the best gift this night?"

The red-beard was already half out his seat when the old man pulled him back down; while the fox-faced one laughed cold and cruel a great shout arose from the town.

"But Brita," said one of her bothersome brothers just then, "Isn't that Ivar's gold privy ring?"

"Be quiet," she whispered. "It must be a mistake; no fool would so mock the gods!"

With a light little laugh the fox-faced stranger jumped up in the center of the head table. "Such a gift, such a gift I never have seen, nor has Odin himself ever seen," he winked. "How shall we choose then, which gift was the best, which deserving of the gods' own good grace? A horse, one that no man living could ride, or the bright shine of gold in your hands?" As he spoke, his fine words burned like fire in the veins; in each man the gold lust did quicken. As he spoke, so he danced, from table to table, leaping boldly across the great fire. "Beast or the gold?" he screamed at the crowd; "The beast or the gold is the best?" The fever was on them, and they shouted right back, *the gold, the gold, the gold!*

"A gift and a curse then," the fox-faced one said, "A gift and a curse, one to each!" To the red-beard he pointed. "A gift for the winner, a gift to our "generous" host." The red-bead's hand fumbled still at his belt, until the old man whispered to him. With a smile that was hard as the stone of the hills, he rose and he started to speak.

"Svalli has given so much of his flock, and his thralls worked so hard in his fields; let my gift to him be the greatest. A fearless goat will I give to him, one as great as an ox of the fields; a goat that can slay any bear, wolf, or bandit, and one that all animals will follow." As he spoke Svalli's eyes lit right up, for he could see he now needed no thralls. With such a goat no herd boys, or guards, no fences or feed, for the wide-open forests could they roam. The goat was led in, all shining and gold, with horns of hard bronze on its head. The goat followed him home, and the flocks did attend, and together did take to the forest.

The roaring and screaming spoke of the fate of the bears, of the wolves and the fanged things that dwelled there. With a glad shout Svalli set about cleaning his house, and he cast every last fieldworker out; not a herd boy or farmer did he let to stay, but each did he cast from his home. With only his body servants remaining, and the promise of riches unshared, did Svalli, giver of the privy ring to Odin's honour, sleep on Walpurgnicht.

But a gift and a curse were promised, not so? At the feast the fox-faced stranger turned with a laugh; to the scarred greybeard he pointed. "And what curse is befitting a wilful young girl who brought lesser gifts to Odin, one who offered a steed unrideable, untameable?"

His one eye flashing the old man did rise, with a scarred hand towards Brita, "For the loser a curse, for a steed on a steed. Let her pony pay the price for her flawed gift of stock. At each mile towards home, and each half, and each quarter, on this night, let her pony lose a shoe. Should one shoe then be lost, let the pony be lost too, fail the once and your pony's life forfeit is too." His voice was cold as ice, hard as steel, and to hear it gave chill to the gold lust that had ere filled the feast. The feast broke up quickly, as each to their beds, until soon were just three strangers gathered around the blot horse. The old one knelt once to stroke the strong neck, whispered, "Worthy," then rose and stalked off.

Brita packed swiftly her wagon and pony, roused her brothers, and bid them ride home in the night. They protested; why not sleep in the hall? But shamed, she could not face her neighbours that night; better wolves and bandits and the long dark road home. As she rode her old pony but a quarter mile towards home, he stumbled, and she knew that he'd thrown a shoe. Mindful of the curse words, she stopped and knelt down, for if she found not the shoe, then her pony would pay. With a sob she threw the lost shoe into the wagon, and led her limping pony again towards the farm. At a half mile, three quarters, a full mile again, did the pony drop shoes as it limped. At a mile and a quarter, at a half mile and three quarters did the pony drop shoes with which it never was shod. At the gates of the steading did it lose its eighth shoe, and she stroked the pony and told him he was shod like Sleipnir that night. In the barn did the boys and the pony both collapse, while Brita alone to the empty home fled.

In her bed, tears of shame did she shed as for sleep did she pray. As she slept, she dreamt of the lord of her dreams, a prince bold and strong, come from far across the waves.

So the giver of the stallion slept that Walpurgnicht.

Came the morning, the mead fumes, the wine fumes burned away, and the men of Hrafnborg thought of events of last day. Some with shame, some dismay, one with something more hot. By this night many things would be clear that were not.

Come the dawn and Svalli had thought of his breakfast, so he whistled for the fearless goat that now served him. From the forest came his flocks, his cattle, pigs and sheep, came his own goats behind, the fearless goat in the lead. More animals now, than he'd had then before, as the wild ones followed his stock from the forest. Svalli laughed at his riches, and eyed one sweet sow, for his bacon for breakfast turned his thoughts just the now. With no stockmen to serve him, no field hands at all, his own hand must slaughter and butcher the sow. With a glad smile he drew steel, and bent down her head; but ere his hand fell did he fall and the reason was this: his gift goat, the matchless, the fearless goat struck. Not wolf, bear, or farmer would harm this goat's flock. His horns struck Svalli; through his doorposts he flew. The goat gave full chase, and his flock chased him too. Through the hall, through the kitchens, and on to his rooms, that goat chased poor Svalli until his backside was blue. The house thralls did flee for the safety of field, as the great home was smashed now by the herds squealing rampage. By noon, bruised and naked, with his house smashed right down, Svalli staggered to town.

Brita roused to shouting unlooked for that morn, as her brothers were screaming and dancing in the barn. Not amused just a bit did she charge out to face them, when what they held caught dawn's light with a soft golden shimmer. Two horseshoes in each hand her brothers did hold; not iron nor nail-scarred but unmarked and golden. Her pony did prance 'round the barn in high spirits, its four hooves still shod in the iron never missing. From the gate came a hail; as Brita did see, a nobleman rode in full company. A Dane-lord who saw her last night at the feast, clad in rich mail with arm rings and a blade scarred with use. Behind him a white mare, beribboned and saddled; a courting gift fit for the mother of princes!

In Jutland was found, in the village of Hrafnborg, two farmsteads of fame. One rebuilding with thralls now well-treated, the other now famous

86

for the warhorses it raises. The oath ring of Hrafnborg is well worth the mention: it is made of two golden horseshoes, welded together.

A Tale of Santa

By John Mainer

In the days long past as Yule approached, each village would gather in the grove, to decorate the tree to Odin, to recall the sacrifice he made for us. At the time of the turning of the sun, they would make sacrifice that Odin's hand be over them still, and the winter have an end. Each family would give offering, each member of the family attend, that the gods could see the praise done them, and give luck to all. In one village in the north was a child bright and fair, who was born with twisted foot. Though her hands were swift and sure, her voice pure and sweet, never had she attended Yule in the village, as she could neither ski nor snowshoe from the steading. Her brothers would tell of the great tree, of the gifts and songs and jests, of the roaring fire, the mirth and company, and she would smile. In time, she grew to fear; the gods never saw her at Yule. They received the gifts of her craft, but not from her hand; and she grew fearful the gods would think she scorned them, and bring her ill luck. While her mother was quick to dismiss this, her father had other ideas. Taking his boys, his axe, and a sledge, he stalked off into the snow. That night he hewed a tree as tall as himself, and dragged it across the fells to the hall. Inside he announced that this year there would be two trees: the village tree in the holy grove, and the family tree by their hearth. If his daughter could not go to Yule, Yule would come to his daughter. All the family thought it grand, and set to with a will.

Mother and sister set about baking and crafting, the brothers to carving and smithing; soon the little tree had everything the great tree in the village would have. When Yule came, the family tromped through the snow to the village grove, leaving only the smiling daughter, with a tree of her own to decorate, and a horn of mead to toast the Yule. That night the offerings were given, in grove and hall, and the gods watched from on high. Odin watched from his high throne, to see his vigil was kept. His ravens Thought and Memory flew above the festivities to see what lay in the worshipers' secret hearts; Odin's wolves Word and Deed coursed the secret places, looking for that we would hide from their master. Odin was pleased, Frey and Freya, Tyr and Thor, and even dour Heimdal were pleased at the splendid offerings, and fine good will of the Yuletide, and they each set their luck upon the land. But the night was not done yet; Word and Deed still coursed the land, and had found what was hidden. In a little hall upon the fells, Odin's wolves did lurk. Word's ears heard the Yule toast given; Deed's eyes saw the offerings bright, by a lamed child with shining heart. Fast as the wind to their master they coursed; for a gift for a gift was his way.

When Odin heard the tale of his wolves, he roared out his laughter at the thought. "A gift," he shouted to his waiting host, "A gift from my hand to hers!" A swanmay cloak he enchanted with a whisper and spun to the admiring hall; bright byrnies that shone like moonlight on silver; swords that flashed like the lightning. Now Frigga laughed, at her dear lord's folly, "What gifts are these for a child?"

"They were good enough for my own dearest daughters," Odin shouted as he waved at his Valkyries' bright steel.

"For a mortal girl, a mortal gift: a smile in return for a smile," demanded Frigga.

"Peace," muttered Odin, seeing her swift-rising ire, "I will find a true gift for this generous girl, before the end of this dark Yule night!"

His boast being given, he strode from the throne, and stalked to Valhalla's dark door. Throwing it wide he stalked through the hall, keen eye seeking just one. A hero who knew how to please little girls, and right quick, for the night was nigh gone. A raven's quick caw drew the Allfather's stare to a fat old Jarl near the fire. With a muttered charm the old Jarl scried the fire, to watch his great grandchildren play. The Battleglad shouted his name with a roar. "Klause, attend me at once!" The old Jarl nigh tripped in his haste, caught his shield and his spear at the run. "You'll not need your weapons or armour this night," spoke the

Allfather in a rumbling chuckle. "I've a girl I need gifted, and this very night; it's my oath to sweet Frigga upon it." With a rune in the hearth the fire did show the lame girl in the steading that night. Klause nodded slowly, and started to chuckle. "Yes, my lord; I've just the thing."

Now the morning was nigh, and the distance was far, so the Allfather gave him some help. He whispered to Klause the smoke charm he knew, to enter and leave through the hearth. He took out his wand, and summoned a mount, a reindeer from Frey's own fair herd, and grave bright runes on each hoof. "Off you go down bright Bifrost, and back before dawn; it's my word you redeem this Yule night."

On the long ride down Bifrost, Klause worked on the gift. Seaman's fingers wove quickly, and he hummed as he worked, for he dearly loved children in truth. The reindeer landed gently upon the roof beams, and Klause slipped gently to the smoke hole. Whispering the Allfather's charm, he turned to smoke, and drifted down into the hearth.

Whispering the counterspell, he swore as he materialised in the fire, and had to put himself out, stomping his fine furs upon the ground. Alarmed, he looked to see the little girl stirring. He looked around for where to place the gift, and then he saw the tree. Klause nodded gently; it was well done indeed, and worthy from such a little girl. He would place his gift beneath hers then, under the tree. Back to the hearth he snuck, oh so quietly. So much fun was he having that he started to laugh, first chuckling, then laughing out loud, "HO HO HO!"

The little girl woke up, alarmed at the laughing stranger in the hearthfire. He was dressed all in furs, and seemed somewhat singed; a great full white beard and a mischievous grin. Touching a finger alongside his nose, his fat turned to fog, and through the smoke hole he rose.

The girl limped to the hearth to touch his boot print, and follow them round to her tree. Beneath the little tree was a bright wrapped shape, and on it was graven her name. The wrap was a sash made of dark green and gold and inside was a wonder indeed. Like a rag doll it was, but trimmed in fox fur. Its hair was braided like hers, but spun from dwarf gold; the dress was bright red and cinched with a belt of gold links. The girl held it close, and started to cry; it was the finest doll she'd ever seen. When her family came home she could not wait to tell of the tree, and the gift giving man.

When next Yule approached, each hall held a tree, the children all offering as sweet as could be. Odin just laughed, but Frigga was not amused; she swore that her lord best keep his word here too.

"Klause!" roared the lord with his eye burning bright, "Get yourself all ready; you'll have a big night!"

But Klause blanched snow white; there were too many kids. "But, my lord, I've not presents for so many kids!"

But Frey heard his cry and sent him some help: he had dwarves unemployed and excesses of elf. With a little assistance he got them all done; now the problem was lifting them; the gifts weighed a ton! "One reindeer won't do it!" he cried to his lord. "He's half loaded now, and collapsed on the floor!"

When Odin attended, it looked pretty grim: the reindeer was buried, with not all the gifts in. Odin took out his wand, and began to incant; he summoned more reindeer, and each did enchant. He summoned not one, not two, three, or four, but just kept enchanting till he had matching fours. Eight magic reindeer, and a rune-carved wood sleigh, "Enough now," Odin said, "To carry the day."

Klause now was loaded, and took to the sky; the sleigh handled nicely, these reindeer could fly! The night passed so swiftly, his work went so smooth, he couldn't help laughing the whole Yule night through. Smooth as it went, there remained now a problem: word of this night had crossed over mountain! From Stockholm to Stuttgart, from the Ode to the Rhine, the word quickly spread of this magic Yule time.